Inferno

Mylia Ashton

Published by Colors of Love, 2024.

Sign up for Mylia's mailing list[1] to receive notification of new releases, ARC opportunities, and other limited communications. Don't worry. Your information is safe and will never be shared.

---

1. https://subscribeto.eo.page/myliaashton

Inferno

Mylia Ashton

Blurb

SPARKS FLY WHEN NICO Martin rescues Elysia Walsh from a fire at her clinic. She has a predictable routine to which she clings. Nico is impulsive and the complete antithesis of her. There's no denying the attraction between them, but when she's determined to avoid commitment, and he's falling fast, their fling could go up in flames.

Chapter One

BLACK SMOKE BILLOWED down the hallway, obscuring Nico's view through his face shield. His peripheral vision tracked two teenagers, one in an exam gown, hurrying toward the clinic's exit, clutching hands and sobbing. He thought about stopping the girls to ask if they had seen anyone else left in the building, but the air of panic surrounding them indicated they wouldn't be responsive.

Seeing they required no assistance, he and his partner moved on, Dawn taking the lead. As they progressed down the hallway, the smoke thickened, settling lower to the floor. He reached for his SCBA automatically as they checked each exam room, quickly but methodically.

At the last room in the hallway, Nico and Dawn stepped inside, dropping to a crouch as they moved through the room, searching for anyone remaining. His low vantage point allowed him to avoid the thickest concentration of the acrid smoke and improved his visibility.

The room appeared to be a laboratory containing various medical paraphernalia, including a microscope, centrifuge, and other gadgets for which he had no name. The room appeared deserted, with a broken vial of blood scattered on the floor, suggesting it had rolled off during a mad rush to get to the door when the bomb went off.

Under that assumption, he didn't expect to find anyone, but indicated with a hand signal to Dawn that he was checking the adjoining room, as procedure dictated. With Dawn behind him, he entered the second room, and his heart stuttered when he saw someone lying facedown on the floor in the corner. Nico moved closer at a rapid pace, identifying the form of a woman when he knelt beside her.

As Dawn joined him, he rolled the pretty black woman onto her back and lifted her in his arms, not taking time to check her vitals. She settled over his shoulder easily. The woman was a negligent burden on his way from the building, and he emerged into fresh air seconds later, his partner close on his heels. Dawn broke off to rejoin the group of firefighters gathered round the engine.

Nico went straight to one of the ambulances, where an EMT waited to care for her. He lowered the woman onto a waiting stretcher and stripped off his SCBA before pushing back his face shield, preparing to find his chief to inform him the building was clear. Nico's eyes fell on the face of the woman, and he caught his breath.

Even the black smudges couldn't disguise her finely honed features. With dark skin and curly brown hair, she was a striking contrast to the crisp white sheet and pillow on the gurney. Even her pink scrubs, decorated with fuzzy bunnies, couldn't detract from her sexual appeal. His groin throbbed with an unexpected jolt of desire, which had never happened to him before with a rescue victim.

Her eyes opened as the EMT slipped an oxygen mask over her face. The rich brown color reminded Nico of pools of molten chocolate. The bewilderment in them made his heart ache. Without removing his elkskin gloves, he took her hand and squeezed gently. "Everything's going to be fine, ma'am."

For a long second, her gaze didn't waver from his. Nico had the sensation she was peering into his soul. He squirmed at the thought, breaking eye contact when he caught sight of the chief. It was a struggle to release the woman's hand, much to his surprise. Glancing down once more, he saw her eyes had closed again. The sound of her harsh coughing remained with him as he made his way to Brady, the chief. Her frightened eyes haunted him, and it took all his willpower to push away thoughts of her and return to the business at hand. Never had he experienced such a connection in such a way, and the woman's image stayed with him as he rejoined the rest of the crew extinguishing the fire.

BREATHING HURT. COUGHING hurt even more, but Elysia couldn't stifle the urge. The oxygen provided some relief from the burning, acrid sensation in her throat and lungs but didn't repress the reflex to clear the congestion. She was vaguely aware of the EMT hovering beside her, monitoring her vitals every few minutes, but couldn't manage to converse yet. Her throat was too raw. Even the thought of speaking made her wince.

The approach of a firefighter, stripped of his Nomex jacket, with a white T-shirt and red Nomex pants, distracted her temporarily from her misery. Elysia's eyes widened when she recognized the blond-haired, green-eyed hunk as the man who had carried her from the building. Her stomach clenched with nerves—or the urge to vomit after a prolonged coughing fit—as he approached, a smile displaying his firm lips, set in a tanned face, to their best advantage.

He tapped the EMT on the arm. "How's she doing, Manny?"

"Pretty well." He pointed to the pulse oximeter attached to Elysia's finger. "Her oxygen is ninety-eight."

"Will you be taking her to the hospital?"

Elysia moved the oxygen mask. "No." She hardly recognized the hoarse voice emerging from her throat.

He turned his attention to her. "How're you feeling, ma'am?"

"Thirsty."

"I can take care of that."

She watched him walk away from her, heading toward the red engine emblazoned with SFD on the side in black letters. The loose fit of his pants hid his buttocks and legs, but the T-shirt clung to his defined arms like a lover, revealing each bulge and flex.

When he returned, water bottle in hand, Elysia quickly dropped her eyes to hide the fact she had been staring. The instant attraction to her rescuer disturbed her. She wasn't the type to have her head turned so quickly, and definitely not just by physical attributes. She tried telling herself gratitude was the only thing she felt for the man, but knew it wasn't true.

"Here you are, Ms.—" He unscrewed the cap before handing her the bottle.

"Walsh. Elysia Walsh." She handed the mask to Manny, nodding to acknowledge his cautionary words of sipping slowly, and took a small taste. The water was like heaven, though tainted by the flavor of smoke lingering in her mouth. After two more small sips, she looked up at the firefighter. "Thank you for the water...and for saving my life."

He inclined his head. "That's my job."

"Still, I want to repay you. May I buy you dinner Friday night?" Elysia's eyes widened at the invitation. What was she thinking? She never dated a man unless she had known him for a decent length of time, knew his character, friends, interests, and flaws. She did not go out with men she had just met, no matter how sexy. She certainly wasn't the one to issue the request. A retraction hovered on the tip of her tongue, but his reply cut it off.

"It's not every day a beautiful woman offers me dinner. How can I say no?" His green eyes sparkled, as if he sensed she had been about to withdraw the invitation.

She couldn't graciously change her mind now. Elysia forced a small smile. "Does Benedict's suit you?"

"If that's what you want." The idea of eating at Sandoval's only fine-dining establishment didn't seem to thrill him. "I'll pick you up if you'll give me your address."

"No." She winced at the panic in her tone, hoping the lingering huskiness masked it. "We'll meet there. Seven-thirty?" She held her breath, expecting him to argue. Hoping he would, and giving her an out from the evening. She wouldn't feel at all guilty for rescinding the invitation should he prove to be forceful or controlling. To her disappointment, he simply nodded.

"I'll see you then." He started to turn but paused, looking down at her. "I'm Nico Martin, by the way." Then he was gone, fading back into the chaos of the scene on the front lawn of the women's health clinic.

She blushed upon realizing she hadn't even caught his name before asking him to dinner. Hormones were to blame for her spontaneous action, which alarmed her further. She hadn't even surrendered to the pull of hormones as a teenager.

It's about time you did, whispered a sly voice in her mind—the voice she was careful to always repress and tune out. This time, it refused to be ignored, whispering all sorts of erotic suggestions about how the dinner date with Nico might end. Much to her surprise, she didn't want to ignore the voice this time.

ELYSIA GROANED AT THE sight in the mirror. Her attempt at sexy had ended up closer to disheveled. Her thick hair, which was so stubborn that only a chemical straightener could tame it, refused to lie sleek after a ruthless flat-ironing session. It was nowhere near the sexy hairstyle she had envisioned.

The black silk pants she hadn't worn for years reminded her why she hadn't worn them with the way they clung to her thighs, accentuating the cellulite she hid under skirts and looser slacks. The gold shirt dipped too low, exposing what should have been generous cleavage on a different woman, but merely accented what she lacked.

Elysia glanced at the clock, biting her lip. She had twenty minutes until she was supposed to meet Nico. Availing herself of valet parking would give her five extra minutes to fix the disastrous sight she currently presented. In record time, she stripped off the slacks and shirt, standing before the mirror in plain white panties and a simple bra, grabbing her hair and pulling it back.

Her hands were adept at forming the bun she wore every day, so that took little time. She secured it with pins and turned to her wardrobe, once again examining her available clothing. Everything seemed wrong, which had already led her to the two sexiest pieces she owned, and look how they had turned out.

With a sigh, she selected a black pencil skirt and a white sweater with subtle threads of silver woven throughout. Adding silver hoops and a chain-link necklace made the outfit dressy enough for Benedict's, though boring. She chose to look on the bright side as she scooped up a silver clutch and hurried from her small house.

Boring was sure to be a turnoff to the all-male Nico Martin, who must be accustomed to dating beautiful women. If he had no interest in her, that saved her the effort of fighting her attraction to him. The thought provided little consolation as she pushed her white Toyota four miles over the speed limit through the sparsely populated streets of Sandoval.

SHE ARRIVED FIVE MINUTES late to find Nico sitting at the bar, watching for her. She nodded to the *maitre d'* on her way through the entryway, sparing no time to admire the heavy wood and antique furnishings of the intimate space. The surroundings were familiar to her.

As she approached, Nico eased off his barstool, drink in hand. He tugged at the tie around his neck, as if unaccustomed to such accoutrements. With a critical eye, Elysia examined him, noting he was sexy in the gray suit but obviously uncomfortable. Her choice of restaurants was clearly a failure.

"I'm so sorry I'm not on time," she said in a rush when reaching him. "I'm never late..." She trailed off, deciding not to elaborate on why she was tardy.

He shrugged. "Don't worry. The beer is cold, and this is a nice place to wait." His expression betrayed the small white lie. Elysia bit back a gasp at the electricity flaring between them when he took her hand. "All that matters is you showed up."

She cleared her throat, resisting the urge to tug her hand from his. The contact discomfited her. Not because he was a stranger, but because she liked it too much. "Are you ready for dinner?"

He nodded as the *maitre d'* appeared at their side, as if psychically summoned. Nico didn't release her hand while they followed the man to a round table draped with a red tablecloth. Gold candleholders shone in the muted illumination from the crystal chandelier above the table. The flames from the red candles provided a cozy glow to accentuate the overhead lighting.

She breathed a sigh of relief when he had to let go of her hand as she prepared to sit at the table. The lightheadedness his touch had inspired almost faded, though she still felt giddy. Inner alarms screamed warnings about his effect on her, but Elysia tried to ignore them as Nico pulled out her chair and seated her. Once again, his touch made her breathless.

Awkward silence fell between them as the *maitre d'* departed after promising their server's attention shortly. She stared across the table, struggling not to stare into his sinfully green eyes while trying to avoid the appearance of rudeness by ducking his gaze. She couldn't strike a balance and ended up looking away.

"Do you come here often?" His mood was difficult to discern. He didn't seem nervous, merely out of his element. Nico's voice didn't betray anything other than mild curiosity.

She nodded. "My uncle owns the place." Elysia didn't share detail that it was technically her step-uncle, brother to her father's fourth wife. The stepmother was long gone, but she maintained contact with Uncle Jacob. "Dad backed him, so he named the place after him."

His brow furrowed. "Benedict Walsh is your father?"

She nodded, struggling to maintain an indifferent façade as she studied him subtly, searching for a hint of avarice. More than once, she had disappointed a suitor who thought she was a ticket to her father's wealth. Due to Dad's propensity to acquire wives like some people collected stamps and coins, his wealth had dwindled over the years—not that she had ever asked for any of it, having wanted to distinguish herself from her mother and Dad's other long line of gold diggers.

"I met Benny once when he stopped to have his driver change my flat tire. Nice guy."

Her heart softened at words. "That sounds like Dad, all right."

The arrival of the waiter prevented further conversation for a moment as they placed their orders. As soon as he moved away, the sommelier arrived within seconds, handing the wine menu to Nico. "What will you have this evening, sir?"

Elysia almost grinned at his deer-in-the-headlight look. It was clear he wasn't a wine aficionado. Smothering her mirth, she said, "I don't believe we'll need a bottle tonight, Jules. Would you please bring me a glass of Sauvignon blanc?"

Jules turned to Nico. "For you, sir?"

"Beer's fine." Nico seemed unbothered by the wrinkling of the sommelier's brow as he left the table.

"I heard they caught the bomber," said Nico after the wine steward had left them.

She nodded, anger bubbling anew. "He's some idiot who didn't bother to research anything. Our clinic only provides health care and birth control. We get government funding, so we couldn't provide abortions even if we wanted to. His statement was meaningless."

"Be thankful he's an idiot." He sipped his beer. "That meant he was incompetent at bomb building, which is why he destroyed the storage rooms and started a fire, but didn't manage to kill anyone."

"Thank goodness for ineptitude," she said lightly, attempting to rein in her anger at the fundamentalist who had tried to kill her colleagues, their patients, and herself because of his ideology that apparently didn't extend to investigating actual providers.

Again, the conversation lapsed. Elysia asked a few meaningless questions, as did he, while accomplishing nothing but killing time. Out of desperation, she asked about his family. That was a topic she rarely broached with a stranger, for fear of having to give reciprocal information, but something needed to move along their exchange.

His posture relaxed, and he began telling her about his large family, all currently living in Florida.

As Nico spoke of his relations, Elysia tried not to let envy plague her. As she laughed along with him at his shared remembrances, she couldn't help contrasting his childhood to hers. Nico's had been full of family and love, while hers was one long stretch of loneliness, filled by a nanny, an ever-changing line of stepmothers and live-in girlfriends, and no siblings. She had some stepsiblings, but none were worth maintaining contact with, so she was alone, except for her father. He was a good man, but too prone to fall in love and chase the next young thing for her to count on him.

As their meal arrived, she asked, "Why are you in Sandoval if your family is in Florida?"

"I wanted to see something besides the East Coast. I ended up here after traveling a few years." He shook his head. "It's funny. I thought I wanted to break away from the family traditions, but I ended up a firefighter just like my brothers, sister, and father, in spite of myself. It just took me a few years longer."

Her eyes widened. "Everyone in your family is a firefighter?"

"Just about." Pride shone in his eyes. Before she could ask anything else, his expression dimmed. "My oldest sister isn't a firefighter now. She married a woman who hated the whole idea, so she gave it up." It was clear what Nico would do in a similar situation. Elysia would hate to be the woman who might ask him to give up his career.

As they ate, they managed to fill the meal with stilted, meaningless conversation. By dessert, Elysia had marked the date as a disaster and was admonishing herself about rash behavior when the bill arrived.

After settling the check, Elysia rose to her feet, not waiting for Nico to pull out her chair. He rose just after her, putting his hand on her lower back as they left the restaurant. She searched for a painless way to close the evening, while getting across the point that she didn't want a repeat. It probably wasn't a concern. What man would want a second date with her after this calamity?

Outside, she handed a slip to the valet, noticing Nico didn't. They stood in silence as the young man brought forth her Toyota. At the curb, Elysia turned to him, extending her hand. "Thank you for allowing me to repay you for saving me, Nico."

His lips twitched, as if repressing laughter. "My pleasure, Elysia." He took her hand, caressing the palm with small circles of his thumb.

With a decisive nod, she pulled her hand from his and slid inside through the opened car door. Elysia looked up at him, trying not to let her eagerness to escape show. "Well...good night."

He nodded but made no effort to walk toward his own car, wherever it might be. She waited for him to speak or move, so she could close the door and drive away, but he just stood there. "Good night," she said again, allowing a hint of exasperation to show.

"I'll follow you home to make sure you get there safely."

"There's no need—"

He tapped on her windshield, already setting off in the direction of the self-parking area. "I'll catch up with you," he called over his shoulder.

She gritted her teeth and resisted the urge to run over him as he stepped in front of her car. No, she didn't want to dent the pristine grill, and blood would never come out of the white paint.

As he jogged away, she slammed the door and shifted into drive, hitting the accelerator with a vengeance. All the way to her quiet home, she seethed with anger at his high-handedness. If he was pulling this stunt to get her to invite him in, he was in for a disappointment.

Yes, he was too sexy for words, but she didn't like his attitude. He was too blunt for her tastes. She had cultivated a sophisticated life, and Nico would never fit into her existence. She couldn't even imagine him in her immaculate brick home, decorated in white with black and gray accents.

She squirmed as an unwanted mental image came to her, of Nico sprawled across her white Egyptian-cotton sheets with his hair tousled, his chest gleaming with sweat and the flush of passion still in his cheeks.

Okay, there was one place he would complement her décor, but she refused to let her self-control slip enough to allow him into her home, much less the bedroom.

Chapter Two

BY THE TIME ELYSIA parked in her garage, Nico's black SUV had caught up with her. He stopped at her curb, bounding out without invitation, to meet her at the door leading into the kitchen.

She pasted on a cool smile, valiantly ignoring the pool of heat that formed in her stomach when he touched her arm. "Thank you for the escort. It was unnecessary, but appreciated."

He chuckled. "You don't lie well, Elysia."

A blush swept through her cheeks. "Pardon?"

"You don't appreciate my chivalry. You're too busy trying to figure out what my angle is." He lifted an arm, resting his palm on the door behind her and bringing himself much closer.

Her spine stiffened. "You're mistaken, Mr. Martin. If you'll excuse me, I'm tired."

"Liar." His breath brushed her cheek. "You're thrumming with need. How long has it been since a man touched you here..." He brushed a hand across her hip. "Or here..." His hand moved higher to cup her stomach before inching up to just below her breast. "Or here?"

Breathlessness made it difficult to speak. "I...I'll scream..."

"No, you won't, because you want this. You wanted it from the moment you saw me." Nico leaned closer still, his lips brushing against her cheek. "Want to know how I know?"

She thought she shook her head, but couldn't be certain. Every nerve in her body responded to his touch, and her brain couldn't seem to coordinate movements.

"It was the same for me." His voice lowered an octave. "From the moment I looked into your eyes, it was like a fist in the gut. I've thought about you all week."

Elysia summoned a reserve of mental clarity. "I haven't thought about you at all. I want you to go now, or I'll have to call the police."

He ignored her, leaning closer still, almost touching her lips with his. "You want me. Why fight it?"

"How can I want you after that disaster of a date? We have nothing in common." She chewed her lower lip, finding it difficult to concentrate with his proximity. "We could never have anything besides a physical connection."

"We have sex in common. Why does it have to be more complicated than that?" He kissed her then, just for a second, but it was long enough to melt her insides. "I don't want a relationship. I saw what love did to my sister. That's the last thing I want."

Finally, they had something other than the physical in common. "I don't want to fall in love either." After seeing the way her father moved from lover to lover so casually, Elysia had decided at a young age she would rather be alone than have a string of affairs. She had maintained her resolve to avoid relationships, never meeting a man worth compromising for.

But it had been so long since a man had held her. Her last lover had been a memory for three years now, cast aside because he wanted a deeper emotional commitment than she would give.

"Great. We know what we want from this. What's the harm?"

She shivered at his breath against her lips. "I don't have one-night stands."

"How about two nights...or a week?" His husky laugh danced along her nerve endings, exciting them to a fever pitch. "Take it one day at a time, and we'll move on when we're no longer hot for each other."

She stared into his eyes, swimming in the molten desire reflected there. Her brain said no, but her body softened against his, and Elysia licked her lips. She cursed her weakness, even as she put a hand on his chest. "Do you want to come in?"

HE SWALLOWED UP THE space inside her home. Feng shui had failed in this instance. "You really like white, don't you?"

Her monochrome scheme suddenly seemed boring next to Nico, and she had to resist the urge to hide the black pillows spread over the white sofa. She owed him no excuses for her tasteful home, she reminded herself. "It's elegant."

Nico shrugged, dismissing the topic. "Coffee?"

She exhaled a breath she hadn't been aware of holding. It had been so long since a man had violated her sanctuary that she had forgotten how the process worked. Had she expected him to leap on her, take her on the floor, and leave? Elysia shook her head at the thought, squashing the ripple in the back of her mind that liked the scenario. "Of course. I have Kenyan dark roast or Raspberry Swirl."

His brow quirked. "Never mind. I'm strictly black, plain."

"Your loss. May I offer you hot tea? Or ice water?" That encompassed her selections, aside from some organic apple-kale juice she was certain he wouldn't want.

Nico scanned her apartment. "Do you have beer?"

She shook her head. "I rarely drink at home."

"Ice water would be great."

She turned to the kitchen, leaving Nico to settle on the sofa. As she peered through the opened top of the Dutch door, she saw him tossing her cushions haphazardly in the corner. Elysia gritted her teeth to avoid saying something. She wasn't fitting the man into her life. Simply her bed.

Her hands shook at the thought, and she dropped the first glass she took from the cabinet. It was a miracle that it didn't break, and she breathed a sigh of relief when she placed it in the stainless steel sink before retrieving another and turning to the refrigerator.

The dispenser hummed, but no ice dropped into the glass when she pressed it against the sensor pad. Frowning, she bent at the waist to examine the dispenser just as the ice burst free, exploding from the chute into the glass, on the floor, and at Elysia.

She slammed the glass onto the counter with more force than necessary and bent to pick up the cubes. How many more signs did she need to know this was a bad idea? What had she been thinking, agreeing to a fling with Nico Martin, a man she had known less than a week? She couldn't allow libido to overrule common sense. Once he had his water, she would explain she had changed her mind and send him away.

With that decision made, Elysia's hands steadied, and she prepared their drinks with no further calamities. Grasping them in both hands, she returned to her living room.

Nico hadn't waited for an invitation to make himself comfortable. He'd kicked off his shoes, removed his jacket and tie and rolled up the sleeves of his light-blue shirt. His sock-covered feet screamed at her from their perch on her antique coffee table. She stared at them when putting his glass of water on a coordinating coaster.

"Thanks." He patted the cushion beside him. "Sit with me."

She eyed the recliner and sat beside him with a soft sigh. Had he read her intentions to maintain distance between them?

Nico took the glass, gulping the water in three long swallows. Elysia watched his throat move, mesmerized by the cords flexing. Her mouth watered as she imagined trailing her tongue across his flesh.

To distract herself, she took a sip of water and choked on it. Nico came to the rescue by patting her back, managing to knock the rest of the water down the front of her sweater. She gasped as liquid soaked her front and then gasped again when Nico's bare hands brushed down her breasts in an effort to remove the ice cubes. She surrendered the glass to him, unable to speak for a moment.

"Come on. You need to get out of that. It's soaking wet." He took her hand, and Elysia stood when he did, following him down the hall. "Which room?"

She opened her mouth to tell him he had done enough, that he should leave now, but a small, "The door at the end of the hall," issued from her. What? Why was she so timid, going along with this? She wasn't that horny, was she?

Her nipples hardened at that moment as heat pooled between her thighs when she ran into Nico's back. Her body reeled from the contact, forcing her mind to admit maybe she was that turned on. She wanted him more than any man who had ever been invited into her bedroom. Why was she fighting it?

He pushed open the door and stepped in ahead of her, whistling through his teeth. "Nice." His eyes were on the blonde sleigh bed, complete with a beige velvet comforter that invited stroking. "I may never leave, darlin.'"

"Tonight only. We agreed."

Nico turned to her, wearing a wolfish grin. "Actually, we agreed for however long it lasts."

Had she agreed to that just by inviting him in? Elysia lifted a shoulder, dismissing the disagreement. He might or might not agree, but they were on a night-by-night basis, with no guarantees.

"Let me help you with that. I'll bet that wool is scratchy when wet."

Elysia stepped away from him, hoping her cool expression hid the heat spiraling through her as her mind conjured up an entirely different use for wool on wet places. "I can handle it."

"I know, but it's more fun if I do it." Nico cocked his head, winking. "C'mon."

She stood still, holding her arms loosely at her sides. The first feather-soft touch of his fingers at the waistband of her skirt made her stomach quiver. She sucked in a breath as he pulled the sweater slowly from the skirt, an inch at a time, until her waist was bared. He moved the sweater higher, revealing her stomach, which quaked continuously as his fingers stroked exposed areas.

"Your skin is so soft. Like milk chocolate. I can't wait to taste it." Nico spoke with an arrogant certainty that he would taste whatever he liked. She didn't contradict him, not wanting to. Now that she had given in to this insanity, she intended to enjoy it fully. What good were morning-after regrets without a worthy night-before?

He pulled the sweater over her head, and Elysia trembled at the hunger in his gaze. It made her feel vulnerable and desirable all at once. Had any man ever inspired such feelings before? Maybe her previous interludes had been so tepid because she knew all about the men selected to be her lovers. There was mystery with Nico, heightening her anticipation. She didn't know what he would do next.

His lips twitched. "A white bra too, Elysia?"

She shrugged. "I like white."

His fingers unfastened the back clasp with confidence, letting the cups lower to just above her nipples. "You need some color in your life, darlin.'"

She shook her head but offered no further protest, too entranced by the way his fingers danced across the silk cups, easing them away from her small breasts with a finesse never equaled by any preceding him. Elysia hardly noticed the bra as it dropped to the floor but didn't miss his fingers caressing her firm brown nipples. They hardened again, straining to meet his fingers, begging for attention. A mingled gasp-groan escaped her when he lightly pinched one. "Nico?"

He met her eyes. "Yes?"

"Kiss me."

She had barely uttered the second word when his arms were around her, and her body melted against his. Elysia tilted her neck to meet his descending head, and their lips touched. She was almost surprised sparks didn't flare when their flesh met. His lips were firm and demanding, but also giving. She molded hers to his, sighing at the electricity humming between them. How could a kiss be so earth shattering?

It only got better when he parted her lips with his and slid inside, playfully pushing his tongue against hers before slipping over the surface. Elysia caught his tongue with hers, pinning it briefly before he broke away.

The kiss changed, getting deeper and more passionate. Nico's hands ventured from her back to her buttocks, cupping and squeezing them as he fitted her pelvis against his. His cock pressed insistently against her pussy, making her dizzy with need.

Nico's mouth moved from hers and took a leisurely trip across her cheek to her ear. Elysia gasped when he twirled his tongue around the tiny hoop in her lobe, darting through the jewelry to lick a sensitive spot. She put her arms around his waist, pressing him closer. He breathed a short laugh into her ear before sucking the lobe and earring into his mouth to bite gently.

When he lifted his head, Elysia surged forward, determined to see if his neck was as tempting as she had imagined. Nico jerked at the first stroke of her tongue down the column of his throat and then groaned when she sucked skin between her teeth to nibble.

"Why do you scrape back your hair? I bet it's gorgeous."

She would have answered it was practical for work, but her mouth was too busy devouring his skin. He tasted sweet, with a hint of salt, and the woodsy fragrance of his cologne contributed to his allure. She didn't hesitate in her appointed task as he unwound her hair from the bun, letting the dark-brown locks fall to the middle of her back in a frizzy mess.

"God, Elysia, I could lose myself in here." Nico brought a handful to his face, rubbing the strands against his cheeks. "I can't wait to see you on the bed, with your hair spread out on the pillow."

"Umm." Elysia kept kissing his neck while her fingers undid the buttons of his shirt to the waistband of his pants. After parting the lapels, she let her mouth venture lower, licking a path across his chest, keeping a hand there to touch the lightly furred skin, running her fingers through his chest hair as her tongue swept over his nipple, eliciting a moan. His hand tightened on her hair, dragging her closer, and Elysia surrendered to instinct.

She swirled her tongue around his nipple in small circles, gradually increasing the radius while still stroking his chest with her hand. Her other hand hooked into his waistband and one finger was bold enough to slip inside to caress his waist.

She cried out with surprise when Nico swung her into his arms to carry her to the bed. He didn't bother to push back the white velvet comforter to reveal the nine-hundred-count cotton sheets underneath. The velvet cradled her back as Nico's body hovered over her front. Her breasts fit perfectly against his chest as he aligned his body over hers. She wriggled, teasing her nipples with the hair on his torso. "You're wearing too many clothes."

He cupped the back of her head, bending her neck to take control of her mouth. "You too," he said, before touching his lips to hers. The kiss was slow, with each stroke of his tongue branding her as his. She was aware of the possessiveness in his actions and reveled in it but refused to focus on the implications of giving him more power in the liaison than she should.

He eased away from her long enough to strip off his shirt, remove his belt and unfasten his pants, leaving the zipper and button of his trousers open. Elysia lifted her hips as he fumbled for the zipper at the back of the skirt, easing the passage of the garment.

Nico touched her thighs, stroking the bare flesh. "I didn't figure you for a garter belt girl."

She squirmed as he ran a thumb over the white garter belt before rubbing the silky hose on her thigh. Should she ruin the illusion and tell him she had resorted to an old- fashioned garter belt and thigh-highs because her last pair of pantyhose had ripped? No. "I need a surprise or two. Keeps things interesting."

"That it does." His hand moved higher, past the garter belt and bare skin, to her panties. They were white too, but he made no comment.

Elysia arched her hips when he ran his thumb down her slit, exciting every nerve centered there. Moisture accompanied the motion, and the panties seemed to chafe unbearably against her folds.

Nico grew bolder, penetrating the elastic side of the panty to caress her skin. "You're so wet."

"I want you." She was going to go insane if he didn't move along soon. She groaned as his thumb slipped inside her, probing her entrance. "Please."

"Not yet."

She gnashed her teeth when he pulled away again, this time to remove her panties. She reached for the clip on one of the garters, but his hand stayed hers. "I'll take care of it." Nico dispensed with the garter belt and panties quickly, leaving only the thigh-highs.

Elysia lay there watching him, wondering what he planned next. Should she take the initiative? She wasn't shy, but there was something so manly about Nico that it precluded her feeling confident enough to demand what she wanted. He might have a dominant personality, but more importantly, he made her want to submit to his whims.

She reached out, running her hand up and down his bicep. "What do you want me to do?"

"Nothing. I just want to look at you." Nico nudged her thighs wider so he could kneel between them. His gaze never wavered from her pussy as he parted it with one hand. The cool air on heated flesh induced a shiver in Elysia, and she held her breath, wondering if she would feel his tongue on her.

Instead, a finger from his other hand circled her clit slowly as he bent forward. His tongue rasped wetly across one of her swollen nipples, teasing her unbearably. He sucked the bud deeper into his mouth as his fingers mimicked the movement to plunge deep into her. Elysia arched her hips, straining for more of his hand.

Nico complied with her unspoken request by thrusting his fingers in and out of her while circling her clit with firm strokes. His tongue laved her nipple, and she squirmed under the passionate onslaught. She was so hungry for him, just aching everywhere. It no longer seemed foolish to rush into a fling. Now, she couldn't get there fast enough. "Please, Nico. I need you."

He lifted his head from her breast but took his time withdrawing from her pussy, stroking her for another minute before relenting. She was slick with need when he stood up to remove his pants. Elysia imagined stroking him, tracing her fingers down the throbbing veins of his shaft and caressing the head as it spasmed against her hand. She watched impatiently as he pulled a condom from his pocket to sheath his length before returning to her.

Nico took up the same position between her thighs, stretching out atop her. He didn't allow his full weight to rest on her as his hand parted her to guide his shaft inside her. Elysia cupped his buttocks, pulling him in as deeply as she could. Her body accepted the length of him with surprising ease considering how long it had been since she had taken a lover.

She arched her hips, meeting his first thrust. The pace was slow, inciting a surge of desire that built in ever-increasing pulses. Elysia's nails formed half-moons in the flesh of his buttocks as he thrust in and out of her, met eagerly each time by her. Nico's hand slipped between their bodies, his thumb seeking out and stroking her clit in time with his thrusts.

His cock was deep inside her, seeking to learn every inch of her channel while his fingers memorized her clit. Elysia cried out when Nico buried his mouth against her neck to bite her with more vigor than tenderness. His roughness excited her, much to her surprise. She was used to polite lovemaking, not the uninhibited variety that Nico seemed so adroit at.

She closed her eyes, struggling to contain a cry of pleasure as she contracted around him. Convulsions swept through her, emanating from deep in her womb and squeezing him to milk every last drop of satisfaction from him. The world looked fuzzy when viewed through the haze of passion obscuring her vision, and her breathing was heavy. It was difficult to draw in a deep breath as she hovered on the edge of coming, just before plunging forward. A cry escaped her as her body went rigid with release.

Spasms shook her, making her contract even tighter around his cock, which spasmed in time with the tremors racking her body. Elysia tried to drag him inside her by digging her nails even deeper into the skin of his buttocks as afterglow started the process of making her muscles relax.

He stiffened against her, thrusting frantically a couple of times before staying deep inside her. Nico seemed to make no effort to conceal his husky groan of fulfillment as he let loose his satisfaction. His cock released in spurts that filled her with contentment, renewing milder spasms inside her core. Their bodies shook in time with each other for what might have been seconds or hours, uniting them as one for that short time.

When it was over, he didn't withdraw from her. Nico turned on his side, bringing Elysia with him, and tucking her body close to his. He brushed a kiss across her forehead, murmured, "Thank you," and held her.

How did she respond? She wanted to weep with the pleasure he had given her. Never had it been so good. What about Nico completely fulfilled her when no other man had?

As he slipped into sleep, emitting soft snores, Elysia cautioned herself to be careful. Nico was dangerous to her ordered life and sheltered heart. If he could breach her body so easily, what could he do to her carefully controlled emotions?

Chapter Three

ELYSIA AWOKE ALONE, finding a note and the slight indent his head had left on the pillow the only proof he had been there. That, and the minor aches of gratification. The twinges were more pronounced when she leaned forward to retrieve the note.

Sorry I can't be here when you wake up, but I had an appointment I couldn't cancel. Be ready at seven. We're doing things my way tonight.

Nico

She frowned at the note, questioning the veracity of his vague appointment. Had it been an excuse to leave, to avoid the awkward conversation that might have awaited him if he had been there when she awoke? His high-handed tone didn't please her either. How dare he issue a dictate? She should make plans with someone else tonight to be gone when he came around. That would show him she wasn't at his disposal.

Elysia knew she wouldn't stand him up as she climbed from the bed, ill-at-ease from her nakedness. The T-shirt she normally wore to bed lay over the white armchair in the corner. For however long this fling lasted, the old T-shirt could stay there. He was too intoxicating to cut short this...whatever it was...prematurely.

Refreshed by the previous night, she strolled to the French doors and opened them, squinting as sunshine flooded the room. Still naked, she took a step onto her balcony to survey the neighborhood. It wasn't quite eight, but several neighbors were engaged in weekend chores as children played on the streets.

She leaned against the wooden rail, hugging her arms over her breasts, wondering what prompted her to stand outside in the nude.

The others in her conservative, upwardly mobile neighborhood would be shocked if they looked up at her balcony and saw her like this. They'd be even more shocked, might even shun her, if they knew the local nurse and heir-apparent to the richest man in town had spent all night in bed with a man she hardly knew.

A giggle escaped Elysia, and she clapped her hand over her mouth, alarmed by the blithe sound. It brought a return to sanity, and she hurried inside, closing the French doors behind her. For a moment, she had been a free spirit, which wasn't like her at all. What had she been thinking?

Last night's decision to end things with Nico at a one-night stand had been a good one. If she was going to be crazy enough to see him again, even for one more night, she had to keep her impulses in check, for fear that she become too much like the women who had paraded in and out of her life over the years. Her own mother had been a gold-digging floozy who had absconded with a hefty divorce settlement and not a backward glance for her toddler daughter.

Shaking her head with disgust at the very idea of being like that woman, Elysia padded into the bathroom, intent on showering and slipping into clothes as soon as possible. Naïvely perhaps, she believed she could conceal the secret thoughts plaguing her mind simply by hiding her body under garments.

AGAINST HER BETTER judgment, she was waiting for Nico by six forty-five, pacing the house, pausing every few minutes to stare at the grandfather clock in the entryway, mutter under her breath and mentally chastise her foolishness once more.

Her internal cautions to be sensible did nothing to slow her racing heart when her doorbell rang at seven. With features schooled in a composed arrangement, Elysia opened the door to Nico and forgot how to breathe. The black T-shirt hugged his arms and torso indecently, revealing every flex and bulge as he moved. The faded jeans, now a worn gray, clung to his legs like a second skin. Her hands itched to test the fabric to see if it was as soft as it appeared. She knew from experience that underneath she would find rock-hard flesh.

"You look delicious," he said, stepping over the threshold without waiting for her to issue an invitation. Nico leaned forward to kiss her, lightly stroking her lips with his tongue. Straightening, he towered over her again, so close she could feel his body heat.

She longed to melt against him but held herself erect by sheer willpower. "Thank you." Did he really consider this white sheath delicious? Bought to wear to an Easter service she had planned to attend with an ex-lover, the dress had gone unused when they had split days before the holiday.

He nodded. "Too dressy though. Do you have jeans?" Before she could respond, he said, "Go change."

Elysia glared at him. Now was the time to nip his bossiness in the bud. "Don't be so patronizing. I've been making my own decisions for a long time, so I don't need your input on my wardrobe."

Nico's eyes widened. "Sorry, darlin'. I meant nothing by it. I want you to be comfortable. Where we're going, jeans are the norm, but it's up to you."

Put like that, her anger faded. "I'll be right back." Elysia returned to her room, half-expecting Nico to follow for a repeat performance of last night. To her disappointment, as she slipped on her sole pair of blue jeans, still stiff with newness, he never made an appearance. She deliberately loitered over selecting a top, hoping he would come in, but he didn't.

With a sigh of disgust at her actions, she chose a white square-necked tunic made of a gauzy fabric, suggesting more than it truly showed, while simultaneously slipping her feet into loafers. When she found Nico in the living room, he whistled. She extended her arms, doing a complete circle. "Does this meet your approval?"

"You bet, darlin'." He stood up, putting an arm around her waist on the way to the door. His hand slipped inside her back pocket, and he winced. "Those jeans sure are stiff, unless your ass is that firm."

His words should have appalled her but instead she had to stifle a laugh. "They're new. I've only worn them once. I pretty much live in my scrubs during the week and casual clothes on the weekend—unless I'm visiting Benedict's."

He made no further comment as they left her house until Elysia headed in the direction of her Toyota. He tightened his grip on her pocket, steering her left, to a gleaming yellow motorcycle parked at the curb. "We'll take my Ninja."

Elysia was already shaking her head even as he continued to bring her with him across her front lawn. "I've never ridden one before."

"It's about time, don't you think?"

"No, I—"

He ignored her objections by thrusting a helmet into her hands. "Try this on for size, Elysia."

"Nico, I'm not riding on this—" She gasped when he pushed the helmet on her head, squashing her bun.

He pushed up the face shield and leaned forward to steal a kiss. "Live a little." His eyes twinkled. "Unless you're scared?"

Hell, yes, she was scared, but not about to admit it. Elysia firmed her trembling lips, nodded just once, and cinched the strap of the helmet under her chin. "Let's go."

Nico's laugh was rich with joy and too contagious. She had to bite her tongue to keep from chuckling along with him. At least the moment of mirth tempered her nerves, and she was almost relaxed by the time Nico put on his helmet and directed her to sit on the seat behind him after he climbed on.

Her hands shook when she grasped his shoulders to steady herself while mounting the seat. The position was odd, and she clutched him tighter when he started the motorcycle. The Kawasaki seemed to roar like an injured beast, and she was two seconds from backing down from his challenge when he shifted into gear and took them onto the road.

Elysia's eyes widened with shock when the vibrations of the seat transmitted to her pussy. Without thought, she shifted positions to feel more of the power, loosening her death grip on Nico's neck in the process.

She spared a glance for the road, deciding she didn't like the way the lines whipped by with nauseating quickness, but otherwise enjoyed the ride. It was difficult to remain in fear for her life when the engine's vibrations kept her constantly aroused, just shy of an orgasm.

Nico detoured from Main Street to an area of town she'd never frequented. If any place in Sandoval could be considered seedy, it was the strip of establishments on Route 24. Her apprehension grew when he slowed down the bike to turn into Blatt's, a local tavern with colorful clientele. She'd never been inside, but rumors abounded of drunken brawls, marriage-ending events, and other horrors taking place there every night of the week. No decent citizen would step foot inside.

All those thoughts ran through her mind when Nico parked by the door beside a beaten-up black motorcycle, but she didn't utter a word when he helped her from the bike and removed her helmet. She had taciturnly agreed to let Nico set the rules for tonight. It was too late to argue now. She just hoped they survived the night without anyone connected to the clinic or her father seeing her at Blatt's.

As Elysia took a seat at a table shrouded by shadows in the corner of the room, she swore she could still feel the vibration of the engine through her body. Her damp pussy throbbed in time with her heart, seeking release. Would anyone notice if she pushed Nico down across the table and had her way with him right there? Surveying the dim interior, clouded with smoke, thick with partiers, she couldn't say with absolute certainty they would. It was the sort of place one could do just about anything without having the other patrons look askance.

"What would you like?"

"Chard...beer, please." When in Rome...

Elysia's gaze remained on Nico's tight form as he moseyed up to the mahogany bar to place their orders. Her eyes narrowed when a redhead sitting on a stool gave him an enthusiastic greeting that included a wet kiss on the lips. Was she jealous of the bimbo? How could she be, considering she had no emotional ties to Nico?

Nonetheless, the sting of jealousy bit into her when the blonde climbed off the stool to plaster herself against Nico. Elysia bunched her hands into fists atop her thighs, fighting the urge to march over and rip every bleached hair out of the slut's head.

Her strong reaction jarred Elysia back to reality. She wasn't the kind of woman to get into a barroom brawl, especially over a man she had spent just one night with. Her anger switched to a simmer as Nico brushed off the woman, got their drinks and returned to the table. She struggled to hide any hint of how she felt behind an aloof smile when he sat down.

"You didn't say tap or bottle, so I took a guess." He pushed a mug of draft beer across the scarred black table.

She lifted it, took an enthusiastic gulp, and managed to hide a grimace of distaste. "Who was the woman at the bar?" Her frosty tone pleased her.

A hint of red might have tinged his cheeks. It was difficult to tell with the low lighting. "Um, a friend."

"You should have invited your *friend* to join us. I hate for her to be alone."

Nico shifted, looking uncomfortable. "I'm sure Annie won't be lonely long."

"Hmm." She took another sip of the beer, finding it easier to tolerate with each drink. "What do you do here, besides drink?"

"Dance, play pool." He shrugged. "Hang out."

She wasn't accustomed to hanging out. Elysia liked plans for everything. She always knew which movie she was going to watch at the theater before going, always reserved activities well in advance when going on vacation, and never changed her mind about anything at the last minute. Drumming her fingers on the table, she scanned the bar again, noticing one of the pool tables was free. "Teach me how to play pool." What she really wanted to do was request he take her home and fuck her until she forgot her own name, but held back. They were having a civilized fling, which included the pretense of dating.

"Sure. Go hold the table, and I'll get the balls from Bill."

Elysia took her mug with her to the table and stood by it with a hand on the edge, not sure if she was holding it properly. This time, Nico picked a spot several stools down from Annie as he conversed with the mid-forties man behind the bar. Soon, he returned with pool balls.

As he racked them, he asked, "You've never played?"

"No." Her father had a billiards table in his game room, but she'd never given it much attention. "It never appealed to me. Until now."

"Fair enough. I'll let you break."

"Break?"

"Grab a cue and go to the other end of the table."

When Elysia had selected a white and blue cue from the wall and stood on the opposite end from Nico, he rolled a white ball to her. She had seen enough on television to know to chalk the cue. After finishing, she figured out where to put the ball and assumed breaking was the act of scattering the balls after he took away the rack holding them.

The cue was clumsy in her hands as she maneuvered it into position to hit the ball. Before she could make her shot, he moved behind her, standing so close she could feel his cock pressing into her buttocks. "Now what?" The breathless question sounded coy, not logical, as she had intended.

"Don't clench the cue so tightly." He put his hand over hers, loosening her grip while repositioning her hold. His other hand rested briefly on her hip before taking possession of her free hand, which he placed on the table, positioning it exactly. "Rest the cue here, but lightly.

You want to be unrestrained when you shoot." He kept his hands over hers, demonstrating the way she should shoot. "Keep your motions fluid."

To her disappointment, Nico withdrew to let her make the shot. As soon as he stopped touching her, she forgot everything he had shown her. The cue barely touched the ball, sending it only a couple of inches off its straight course, without getting anywhere near the pyramid of balls at the other end of the table. She groaned, ready to quit.

"My turn." Nico took a cue and held it with confidence born of practice. Elysia's eyes didn't stray as he leaned over the table to make his shot. The way his buttocks clenched in the tight jeans dried out her mouth. The beer she gulped did little to provide relief but kept her from uttering a moan when he completed his shot, making his body one streamlined work of art. The kind meant to be touched, not hung on a wall and admired from a distance.

The cue ball scattered the others when it slammed into their midst, causing three to drop into pockets immediately. He looked over his shoulder. "It's still my turn, but why don't you go ahead?"

She shook her head, in no hurry to end his turn. He was delicious enough to watch all night. "Play by the rules."

He started to walk past her but turned to pull her against him and press his mouth to hers. Elysia's first thought was of protesting the public kiss. Her second was all about the kiss itself. She wrapped her free arm around his waist, trying to pull him closer. His mouth devoured hers as his tongue feathered against her lips.

When he pulled away, his grin was full of smug arrogance and a healthy dose of satisfaction. "Darlin', I've always found it more fun to break the rules." He moved past, leaving her with a lingering squeeze on her bottom.

The balls seemed to disappear with lightning speed as Nico set about putting them into the pockets. She watched with rapt attention each time his muscles bunched or flexed, studied his expression for clues of his mood and felt the moisture in her pussy spread. By the time he knocked the eight-ball into the corner pocket, a light sheen of perspiration misted her body and she was lightheaded with arousal.

"Another?" he asked, rounding up the balls from under the table, where they had dropped after going into the pockets.

She shook her head. "Where's the ladies' room?"

"Down the hall." He pointed to a sign across the room. "Are you sure? You didn't get to play much."

"It's fine." She abandoned her beer and rushed to the restroom, shaking with the effort not to make a fool of herself. Her body ached for his. She was hotter than she had ever been, dripping with need. A few minutes of privacy was all she needed to collect herself. She hoped.

The restroom was as dim as the rest of the bar but not as smoky. There were two stalls, and she chose the handicapped one because it was closer. Elysia locked the door and leaned against it, taking deep breaths that did nothing to calm her. This night had been nothing but foreplay, and she was ready for the main event. The only thing that had stopped her from begging Nico to leave was she didn't think she could wait to get back to her place.

The main door opened, and she tried to halt her rapid breathing. Her inhalation turned to a gasp when Nico peeked over her stall. "What are you doing? This is the ladies' room."

He grinned, unrepentant. "Open up."

She shook her head, even as her fingers obeyed his command and turned the lock. A flutter of common sense had her reaching for the door as he swung it open. "You can't...we can't."

"Remember the rules, darlin'." Nico entered the stall with her, locking the door. He was too close for rational thought as he pinned her against the side of the stall, pressing his mouth to hers. "Break them," he said, right before kissing her.

Propriety dictated she push him away, but her body had other ideas. Elysia clung to Nico, running her fingers through his hair with one hand while resting the other at his waist. A moan escaped her when Nico's hand slid under the hem of her tunic to caress her stomach. His tongue thrust inside her mouth, and she met it eagerly, parrying his attempts to explore all of her.

One of his hands moved higher, cupping her breast through her bra, while his thumb rubbed over her swollen nipple, inflaming it with the lacy fabric. She nipped his tongue, earning a pinch that served only to heighten her arousal. Her hips arched of their own accord, bringing her dripping pussy against his cock, separated only by the fabric of their jeans. The barrier was too much, and she wanted to strip off their clothes and have him pin her to the wall.

Nico broke the kiss to sweep his mouth down her throat, pausing to bite the bend of her neck with just enough pressure to elicit a moan. Elysia tightened her fingers in his hair, trying to halt his descent as he slid lower. He ignored her temporary resistance, and she stopped fighting when he pushed her tunic above her breasts. His tongue swept into the valley of her cleavage, modest as it was, and he inhaled. "You smell like flowers," he said against her skin, sparking flicks of heat with every breathy word.

"You smell like sex." The blunt words shocked her, but he didn't seem taken aback by her uttering them. And it was true. Nico smelled, tasted, walked, and talked S-E-X. She couldn't help but respond. Urgent hands tugged his T-shirt up so she could caress his abdomen, which fluttered under her hand. His cock pressed more insistently against her pussy through the jeans, and she parted her thighs wider to allow it to nestle deeper.

To her surprise, he shifted her suddenly, pressing her against the wall and supporting her on one of his thighs while she braced her hands on his shoulders. His movements were smooth and quick when he released the back clasp of her bra and pushed the cups above her breasts, along with the tunic. Once freed, her breasts strained for his touch, and Elysia's nipples tingled with warmth.

Nico's mouth was gentle, but with a hint of roughness, when he took possession of one nipple. The bead disappeared into his mouth, where he flicked his tongue over the tip, causing her to stifle a cry of passion. Elysia dug her nails into his shoulders, pulling him closer still while writhing against his thigh, seeking relief for the inferno blazing inside her pussy. "Nico, I can't take this." They had to leave, find the nearest bed and satiate each other.

He lifted his head to stare into her eyes. "Yeah, you can, darlin'. Trust me." Then his hands moved to her waistband, dispensing with the button and zipper to plunge his hand inside. His fingers stroked her pussy through the silky panties she wore, and Elysia tossed her head from side to side, desperate for relief, as his fingers teased her clit through the silk. "Please, Nico. Let's get out of here."

"Easy." His hand left her pants, and he lowered her back to her feet. Elysia experienced a dart of disappointment, despite it having been her request to stop and find somewhere else more private. Her discontent changed to confusion when Nico got on his knees before her.

Her eyes widened when he pulled down her jeans and panties. Somehow, she managed to remain coherent enough to kick off her loafers and step out of them.

There was no mistaking his intentions as he leaned forward, tongue extended. She twined a hand in his hair, not sure if she wanted to push him away or pull him closer. He didn't allow her to choose, lunging forward suddenly, tongue seeking out her heat. Elysia closed her eyes with a gasp, leaning against the stall wall for support, as Nico's tongue sought out all her secret places, paying special attention to her clit, swollen with need.

The moist swipes of his tongue probing her opening made Elysia ball her hands into fists to keep from shouting. Nico pressed his tongue deeper inside her pussy. She shifted with restless energy, needing more than his intimate kiss. She wanted him inside her.

Nico seemed to have read her thoughts, because he brought a hand between her thighs. His tongue abandoned her opening, leaving her temporarily bereft, until two of his fingers plunged inside to take its place. It wasn't his cock, but the digits were almost enough to satisfy her. When Nico swirled his tongue around her clit, she cried out while mindlessly thrusting against his face as spasms in her pussy built in intensity.

She was on the brink of release when the outer door opened. Elysia's eyes snapped open, and she froze as footsteps went past their stall, though Nico continued to lick her pussy. She pulled on his hair, trying to get his attention, but he remained focused on his task. "Nico," she said so quietly she barely heard it herself as the door to the stall beside them closed and the woman engaged the lock.

She couldn't help but see Nico kneeling on the floor and know what they were doing. Shame burned through Elysia, firing her cheeks, but another sensation fought for supremacy. It was the wild impulse to ignore the other woman's presence, and it was winning. Nico's passionate ministrations, continuing without pause, helped it along toward victory. With a sigh of defeat, she closed her eyes, struggled not to breathe too heavily, and let his tongue work its magic.

The woman was in the process of washing her hands when the orgasm swept over Elysia. Try as she did, she couldn't keep in a moan of satisfaction. Every muscle in her body quivered with release, and she slumped against Nico, who was still caressing her with slow strokes, coaxing every drop of pleasure from her.

The outer door closed, bringing Elysia back to a semblance of awareness as Nico got to his feet. Her actions should shock her, and they did, but she was too limp with gratification to make an issue of what they had done.

He kissed her gently on the mouth before saying, "That was intense. There's a real wanton underneath that schoolmarm exterior, Elysia."

"Only with you," she admitted, leaning against him with her arms on his shoulders. His hands moved between their bodies to free his cock from his jeans. Elysia kept her head against his chest as he ripped open a foil packet taken from his pocket and covered his cock.

Her thighs parted wider when he shifted into position, aligning his cock with her pussy. With a soft gasp, Elysia welcomed him fully inside. After the last orgasm, she didn't know if she could survive another, but he set about proving she could, using his cock and hands to stroke her to a fever pitch. As her pussy contracted around him, she tossed her head, biting hard on her tongue to hold in a cry.

Nico filled the silence with a groan as he came, pulling her so tightly against him that they were almost one person for a moment, especially when their heartbeats thundered in time with each other.

When it was over, he held her for a long moment before pressing a kiss to her neck. "Your place or mine?"

She was exhausted and opened her mouth to tell him she couldn't do this again tonight, needing time to recover, but her answer caught her by surprise. "Yours. I want to see where you live."

"It's your standard bachelor pad, but it has a bed."

"That's all we need."

AS HE'D SAID, HIS APARTMENT was standard fare—white walls, brown carpet and a single bedroom, which they didn't make it to. As soon as Nico closed the door, he swept Elysia into his arms and carried her to the overstuffed leather sofa. She stretched out on the sumptuous cushions, supporting her head on an arm bent behind her. She smiled up at him as he stood over her. Her eyes focused on the bulge in his pants, and she licked her lips.

Nico settled onto the couch, straddling her, making his cock dig into her stomach. He braced his hands on either side of her head and leaned forward to kiss her. Elysia opened her mouth when his lips touched hers, changing the kiss from casual to intense by sweeping her tongue inside his. She brought both hands forward to splay across his chest, pulling him closer.

Nico groaned when she sucked his lower lip into her mouth, and she grasped handfuls of his shirt to keep from vocalizing her own pleasure. Her pussy ached with need, despite the pleasure he'd already given her, and she arched her hips, finding no gratification in empty space.

Frustrated, Elysia tore her mouth from Nico's before he could pin her tongue with his. "I want you." It was liberating to be so blunt with her emotions. So liberating, she tried it again. "I want your cock inside me."

Nico seemed surprised by her words but nodded. "Sure, darlin'. Whenever you're ready." He winked.

Elysia couldn't hide a grin of satisfaction at his startled look when she shoved against his shoulders. He went tumbling off the couch, and she followed, now straddling him as they lay on the floor. She tugged at his T-shirt. "Now would be appreciated."

He groaned. "Can I have a minute to catch my breath? That was a helluva ride." "No, but it will be." She ignored his requests to take it easy as she pulled at his shirt until it was over his head. When he was bared from the waist up, she let her hands roam over his chest, raking her nails across his nipples. She enjoyed his sharp inhalation so much she scratched the tender nubs again.

"Damn." He didn't sound angry. Rather, surprise and something more colored his tone. Enjoyment, perhaps?

Elysia bent her head so she could focus her attention on the button and zipper of his jeans. They yielded to her determined hands with a rasp, and she opened the pants to reveal her prize. Nico's underwear posed a slight deterrent, and she had to tug at the waistband of his jeans and briefs a few times until he cooperated by lifting his hips.

In her impatience, she got the pants no lower than his knees. Seated across his shins, she shifted slightly to maximize her mobility. Then Elysia looked up at him, finding Nico watching her with amused indulgence. She wanted to wipe that expression off his face, wanted him to feel the same need she had, just as urgently. She hated being vulnerable, but if she was going to be, she refused to experience it alone.

"I'm going to fuck you now," she said, almost conversationally. He folded his hands behind his head. "Is that right?"

She nodded just once.

His grin held more than a small measure of self-satisfaction. "Wouldn't you be more comfortable on the bed?"

"I'll be plenty comfortable on your cock," she retorted.

A hearty laugh escaped him. "By all means, go for it. I'm not going to stop you."

"No, you aren't." He still wasn't feeling the same urgency, but that was about to change. Elysia leaned forward, catching a brief glimpse of his stunned expression just before his face disappeared from her line of sight. He jumped when her lips touched the head of his cock, but she spared no mercy for him to adjust to the erotic intrusion. In a smooth motion, Elysia engulfed his cock in her mouth, somehow accommodating all of him.

He tasted like come and latex, along with something uniquely him. It wasn't completely unpleasant, and she soon forgot her initial reaction to his flavor when his cock convulsed in her mouth. She began to suck, working her head up and down, and knew she had provoked the response she wanted when he started pumping his hips.

Elysia had her hands braced on his thighs, but she brought up one to hold the base of his cock, squeezing lightly. Nico groaned when she moved her mouth in a circle around his shaft, applying more suction to the head.

His thrusts increased in speed, and he sounded hoarse when he spoke. "I'm about to come, darlin'. You're too good."

She bit him on the head, scraping her teeth across the sensitive flesh. When he uttered a wordless protest, she lifted her head to smile at him. "You aren't coming yet."

He growled, glaring at her. "Are you playing with me?"

Elysia didn't respond verbally. Instead, she let her gaze settle on his cock while her hands dispensed with the tunic. Nico reached up to help with her bra, and she smacked his hand lightly. "This is my show, Nico."

He laughed, though it contained more strain than amusement. "I guess I'll just watch."

"For now." She unfastened the bra and tossed it onto the floor beside the tunic. Her sense of order winced at the mess, but desire overrode her natural prissiness, and she turned her attention to the jeans. Her hands shook with anticipation, making it slow work to strip her jeans and underwear down below her knees. Though they restrained her legs, she had no time to waste getting them off.

"Condoms?"

Nico pointed downward. "Right pocket of my jeans."

Elysia reached behind her awkwardly, feeling for a bulge in the denim. When she found the pocket, she plunged her fingers inside and pulled out three condoms. With haste, she tore one off the roll. It resisted opening so she used her teeth. Her urgent need was disquieting, but she was too immersed in it to back off, cool down and think about all the reasons why she shouldn't be attacking Nico—least of all, she wasn't like this. Clearly, she was when with Nico.

His cock jerked at her feathery touch when she rolled the condom down the shaft. Elysia paused to caress his head, applying a small amount of pressure to the sensitive V until he lunged upward, his teeth clenched. Satisfied he finally felt the same driving desire as she did, she scooted higher up his body.

If not for the jeans hindering her legs, she could have been on him in seconds. It took close to a minute to position her pussy atop his cock and get a sense of balance. When she was centered, Elysia sank down on him, and they both moaned when his cock filled her.

She dug her nails into his chest where she'd braced them and began arching up and down. "That feels so good." Elysia circled her hips while clenching her pussy around his cock.

"You've got that right, darlin'. I could stay in your hot little pussy for hours."

A bead of sweat dripped into her eyes, but she didn't bother to wipe it away. "I can't wait that long."

"Me neither," he admitted with a grunt while driving forcefully inside her. His cock spasmed, making her womb quake in response. Elysia was on the edge of coming, and when she scooted forward a smidge and arched her back, his cock rubbed right against her clit as she rode him. Their frantic thrusts pushed them closer to the edge, and she suddenly found herself falling over it.

The heat of his liquid satisfaction spread to her through the condom as he climaxed, and it triggered more convulsions in her pussy. She tightened her muscles around his cock and crested the peak of her orgasm, gradually slowing the speed of her thrusts until the last bit of tension faded, and she collapsed on top of him, breathless.

They didn't speak, and she was grateful not to have to make conversation. At that moment, she was still out of control, a sensation that terrified her. She needed time to gather her composure, which was impossible with his cock slowly waning inside her. After the way she had just behaved, she couldn't face him and act normally. It was better to hide her face against his chest and try to forget how wild she had been. That was easier to plan than execute with her body still glowing from the amazing release, and her inhabitations temporarily freed from restraint.

She knew, lying atop him, that she couldn't let this happen again. If he could make her lose control this way, she could easily end up like her mother. Elysia couldn't allow herself to lose her hard-won self-respect to desire.

But when his cock hardened a few minutes later, and his hands cupped her breasts to rub her nipples, it never occurred to her to refuse him. In a matter of moments, she was swept away again, forgetting her previous resolutions.

42

Chapter Four

NICO WAVED OFF THE last of the guys trying to talk him into going to the bar while dialing Elysia's number. He hadn't seen her in the three days he had been on duty, hadn't even called her, but hadn't been able to think about anything except her during that time. The last two weeks of their affair had flown by, it seemed, and he still hadn't gotten enough of her.

It scared the hell out of him, but here he was, calling her after only three days of self-imposed silence, when he had been trying to make it a full week. Would she be happy to hear from him or irritated he had gone so long without speaking to her?

He grimaced as the phone rang, reminding himself she hadn't tried to call him at the station either, though it would have been a simple matter of looking up the number in the phone book. Perhaps she was managing to compartmentalize their casual fling better than he was.

She answered on the third ring, rasping, "Hello."

"Elysia?"

"Yes. Nico?"

"You sound awful." He winced at his honesty.

"Thanks." She coughed before continuing. "I picked up a bug at the clinic, I guess." It had officially reopened at the beginning of the week.

"I was going to bring by Chinese food, but maybe I'd better bring you soup instead." Smooth invitation. He shook his head at the way the words had emerged, leaving her little choice.

Silence filled the line for a moment. "I'm sick."

"I won't catch anything." It was clear from her tone she was trying to get rid of him, so why wasn't he accepting that gracefully?

Again, she hesitated, finally saying, "I'm not feeling up to anything...if you know what I mean?"

His voice lowered, becoming more reassuring. "That's fine, darlin'. I'll bring food, DVDs, and pampering."

Her reluctance was evident, along with her weariness, when she spoke again. "Fine."

Nico didn't like the surge of relief that swept through him, nor the way his stomach clenched with anticipation at seeing her. He forced himself to sound neutral when replying. "Great. Do you want Chinese food or soup?"

"Egg-drop soup sounds good."

"Right. I'll see you soon, darlin'." Nico hung up before she could retract her acquiescence, sensing she was on the verge of telling him not to come over. He didn't want to scrutinize too closely why he was so desperate to see her or why his experiment of imposing some distance between them had failed. Nor did he want to think about why he couldn't get her out of his mind or how it had hurt to know she thought he only wanted to come by for sex. It was a logical assumption on her part, since every date they'd been on had ended tangled in the sheets of one of their beds, so there was no reason for him to feel wounded.

No reason he wanted to examine anyway.

ELYSIA MADE LITTLE effort with her appearance before Nico's arrival, deciding to let him see her complete with red nose, swollen eyes and an old robe left from college. This sudden move from casual sex into relationship realm alarmed her, maybe because she wanted to move to the next level as she never had before. When a man got too close, she'd had no trouble sending him on his way, but didn't feel the same compulsion to do so with Nico.

Her insides had warmed in a disconcerting way when he'd said he was going to come by just to pamper her. No one had ever brought her soup or taken care of her when she was sick. It was disconcerting to have her casual lover showing such tender concern.

When the doorbell rang, the thoughts were still swirling through her mind as she tried to decide what was the best way to get rid of Nico and her own treacherous longings.

All thoughts of sending him on his way flew out of her brain when she opened the door to see Nico holding a large teddy bear under one arm and a bag of Chinese food in his hand. The bear held a heart that said "Get Well." Before she could school her reaction, she was reaching for the bear, cuddling it against her.

"You like it?" His boyish need to please was evident in his expression and the way he shifted from foot to foot.

Elysia nodded, incapable of speech for a moment. Nico slipped past her to set the Chinese food and stack of Redbox DVDs on the coffee table before turning back to take her in his arms.

Sick as she was, her body responded to his proximity, and it was strange to have him press a chaste kiss to her forehead instead of receiving the passionate greeting she had expected. Somehow, she ended up cuddled against him, with the bear forming an awkward barrier between them. Tears burned at the back of her eyes, and Elysia blinked rapidly to dissolve them, not certain why she wanted to cry.

"C'mon. You should be resting." He guided her to the couch, seating her on the middle cushion. Looking sheepish, he touched the bear briefly. "Silly, huh?"

She shook her head. "It's wonderful." Her voice was wet with suppressed tears, but at that moment, she was unable to hide her emotions and hoped he would chalk it up to her illness. "Thank you."

Nico shrugged, as if trying to push aside his embarrassment. He didn't respond except to remove a Styrofoam container from the plastic bag and hand it to her. "Egg-drop soup." A plastic soup spoon followed before he arranged two boxes of food and chopsticks on the table.

Elysia made a production of opening the soup and examining the contents before taking a small bite, desperate to avoid his eyes lest he see the vulnerability in hers. She only looked up when he called her name, jiggling two rental cases.

"I wasn't sure what you liked, so I picked up a chick flick and an action movie. Which will it be?"

She pointed to the action movie, in no mood to have her already-raw emotions exposed further by any heartrending issue the chick flick might explore. Nico put it in her DVD player before joining her on the couch.

As they watched the movie, eating, no words passed their lips. When Elysia had eaten as much of the soup as she could, she put the lid on and leaned back against the cushion, carefully resting her head on his shoulder. Nico put aside his food to take her into his arms. A spark of electricity arced between them, but his demeanor was one of caretaker rather than lover as he held her.

She relaxed into him, enjoying his embrace more than she should. It was a foreign experience to have someone else care about her wellbeing, to take care of her. That it would be Nico, the man she was supposed to be having a fling with, made it even stranger. He wasn't supposed to be the sensitive type. All brawn with a massive dose of sex appeal—that was his persona. He wasn't supposed to upset her preconceived notions and make her start to fall for him.

Her eyes, drooping before, snapped open at the thought. Elysia tensed, almost pulling away, as if she could escape her emotions just by putting some distance between them. Three days of silence on both of their parts hadn't done anything to diminish her desire for him, so why did she think withdrawing from his embrace would do anything?

"Elysia? Are you okay?"

Slowly, she nodded, allowing her body to relax again. "I was falling asleep."

"Go ahead. I'll make sure you get to bed."

The words themselves were sexy, but delivered in a nurturing manner. Elysia tried to force her thoughts from her emotions to concentrate on the movie, but it was a long time before she was successful.

BY THE END OF THE MOVIE, Elysia was snoring softly against him. Nico looked down at her upturned face, noting the lines of worry around her eyes and wondered what haunted her.

She sighed in her sleep, snuggling closer. A glance at the clock revealed it was nearly ten, which meant he should get going. In other circumstances, he would have stayed with her for a few hours, but tonight, didn't feel the urge.

As he got to his feet, lifting her into his arms effortlessly, Nico acknowledged that wasn't true when his cock swelled against his jeans. He had the desire, but her needs outweighed his wants. Never before had he experienced this curious blend of tenderness and passion for a lover. Not one of the women he had been involved with in the past had ever evoked a need in him to take care of them.

Carrying her to her room, staring down at her, Nico faced an unpleasant truth. He was in love with Elysia. It didn't give him the surge of terror he'd expected. Instead, as he placed her under the covers and brushed a kiss against her cheek, satisfying warmth spread through him, radiating from his heart, not his cock. For the life of him, he couldn't remember right then why he had fought so long against feeling something real for a woman.

"I love you," he said in a whisper, trying out the words and liking the way they sounded. Her eyes opened briefly. She locked gazes with him for just a second before her eyes slammed closed again, and her snoring increased. It was just long enough for him to catch the glint of panic in her eyes.

Chapter Five

AS SOON AS ELYSIA OPENED her eyes the next morning, Nico's words swirled through the layers of her subconscious to lodge in the forefront of her mind. With a smothered groan, she rolled out of bed, desperate to escape her emotions. Panic was there, as it had been last night, but there was more. Was that giddy tickle in her chest happiness or simply the remnants of her cold?

Elysia hurried into the bathroom, trying to deny she felt anything other than fear at Nico's confession. Her eyes revealed something different than her brain wanted to see. They were soft pools of darkness, tinged with a warm glow. Her lips tried to curve into a smile, and she had to school her expression into her most severe look, one usually reserved for the cocky young men who came to her clinic and insisted they didn't need to use condoms even though they'd caught an STD or impregnated a young woman.

Dammit, she was pleased with Nico's words. Somehow, he had wormed his way into her life, burrowing into her heart in a way no man had ever done before. Her walls had dropped, her defenses had let her down...and she didn't care?

"I love you." Her lips formed the words hesitantly, and her voice was a rusty rasp in the enclosed space of the bathroom. She waited for some reaction, like the ceiling to fall on her, but nothing happened, other than a lightening in her chest.

Padding from the bathroom, forgetting about her morning ablutions, Elysia continued practicing the words under her breath. Each time she said them, they came easier, until she almost thought she could say them to Nico when next they met.

HER FLEDGLING COMFORT with Nico's confession and her own response lasted until the next afternoon, when her phone rang. Not given to moments of intuition, it was with strange foreboding that Elysia answered the telephone, every instinct screaming to ignore the out-of-area number. "Hello?"

"Elysia, darling."

Her stomach churned as soon as her father's voice came over the line. "Hello, Dad. How are you?"

"Deliriously happy."

Ah, a new woman. "Oh?"

"I'm getting married."

Elysia's lips curled in a cynical grimace. "You're already married."

Benedict laughed. "Oh, darling, not for long."

"What happened with Henrietta?" Or was it Helena? The number of women who had paraded through Elysia's life as her father's companion were numerous, so it was no wonder she couldn't keep them straight.

Her father sighed, sounding impatient. "She was pushing for things I didn't want to give, Essie."

She winced at the loathed nickname, but let it slide. He wouldn't listen if she asked him not to use it. And she didn't have to ask about what Henrietta might have wanted from her father. It couldn't have been financial, because he was too generous with his wealth for that to bother him.

His wife must have wanted more of his time, or perhaps even a child. She'd overheard him telling one stepmother once that he'd never make that mistake again, because it was too costly. Knowing he loved her hadn't kept that from hurting, at least a little.

"Your solution to that was to find a new wife?"

Benedict's tone sharpened. "I didn't plan it. It just sort of happened, but I help falling for Calista. She's the one. I'm sure this time."

"Hmm."

Not picking up on Elysia's skepticism, Benedict continued. "She's never been married, has no children, owns a chain of restaurants, and she loves to sail. We're going to spend six months sailing around the world for our honeymoon on the new yacht It's a ninety-footer, complete with a full staff—"

Elysia tuned out her father's description of the yacht before he started enthusing about Calista's charms—all physical. The thought of using women so callously turned Elysia's stomach, though she had little sympathy for the women who had married her father, including her own mother.

With the exception of Dad's first wife, who had died long ago giving birth to a brother Elysia would never know, they should have all known what to expect—a few months or years of commitment followed by a fat payoff. Since they seemed to actively seek out her father, she concluded it was more of a business relationship than a marriage on both sides. Even knowing her father embraced a pale mockery of marriage gave her no real desire to experience a truer version.

Nothing good ever came from love. It was a lesson Elysia had learned repeatedly over the years, but a moment of weakness had nearly undermined her. Whatever fragile emotional attachment she had almost allowed to grow had to be firmly squashed.

Her father's phone call and latest marriage was a timely reminder of what Elysia had known most of her life. She was better off alone than allowing herself to love anyone as passionately as she could love Nico. She would lose herself in him, and for what? An emotion that couldn't possibly last. She had to protect herself, and that meant hardening her heart.

NICO POUNDED ON ELYSIA'S door relentlessly, knowing she was home. He had seen her car in the garage when he'd peeked in the window. Her avoidance of him the past five days was about to end. He was going to force a confrontation, damn her wishes and his own fear of rejection. Limbo was worse than knowing how she felt about him, even if her feelings weren't mutual.

Finally, she opened the door, a trace of annoyance in her expression. "Nico? What's so urgent?"

He didn't wait for an invitation, pushing past her. She followed him, emanating arctic silence as he turned to face her in the living room. "Why have you been avoiding me?"

Elysia frowned, giving every appearance of ignorance. "I don't know what you mean. I missed three days of work, and as the only one trained to perform some of the diagnostic tests, I've been struggling to catch up with everything."

"You haven't had time to return even one of my calls in the last five days?" He snorted. "Yeah."

"I had other priorities."

Her cool façade, such a contrast to the inferno burning inside him, was infuriating. He took a step closer, absurdly pleased by the way she stood her ground, though he wouldn't have minded some acknowledgement she wasn't as unaffected as she pretended. "Liar."

Her eyes widened. "Excuse me?"

"You're running scared." Nico shook his head. "It won't work. You have to face me sometime."

Elysia turned partially away from him. "I have no idea what you're talking about."

He touched her shoulder, and she tensed at the light contact. "I know you heard me."

She shrugged him off. "Heard what?"

He pressed her back against his chest. "I told you I loved you."

Elysia shook her head. "No."

"I did." He turned her resisting body so she was facing him, though she avoided his gaze. Nico lifted her chin, forcing her to look into his eyes. "I do. I love you."

Fear flared in her eyes. "You're crazy. You don't know me."

"I know all I need to."

She pulled away. "No, you don't. You don't know anything important about me. Did you know my father has been married seven times...about to be eight? There was also a never-ending line of his girlfriends in my life, always a priority over me." Tears leaked from the corners of her eyes, and she brushed them away with an impatient gesture. "Falling in love is for fools."

"Then I'm a fool, because I love you." Nico reached for her, not allowing her to shove away his hands. He pulled her stiff body into his arms. "Just give me a chance to prove I'm not like your father."

"I know you aren't, but it doesn't matter now. The past taught me an important lesson. I don't want to love a man, and I don't want one to love me." Her expression was a perfect sheet of ice when she looked up at him. "I don't want your love, Nico. You're wasting your time trying to convince me."

He shook his head, refusing to believe. "You don't mean that. It's natural to be frightened after the experiences in your childhood, but I wouldn't hurt you."

"I know, because you'll never have the chance." Elysia withdrew from him, pointing to the door. "You need to leave now."

"Elysia—"

"Go. I don't want to see you again."

Nico stared at her for half a minute, searching for a crack in her veneer, but finding none. His shoulders slumped, and he took a step toward the door. "You'll change your mind. You just need time to think things through."

Elysia turned away from him. "I won't. I don't want you, and I definitely don't love you."

He winced at the pain her words caused. Nico had the fleeting urge to rage at her, but it faded quickly. Nothing he could say would reach her right then, emotionally frozen as she was. He could only hope she might come to her senses and open up to him in the coming days. His happiness—and hers—depended on it. He walked away without looking back, not wanting her to see the tears misting his eyes, wondering if she was as close to weeping as he was. In her frigid state, he doubted it.

Chapter Six

ELYSIA POURED A CUP of coffee, deliberately avoiding the gaze of Cleo, the other nurse on shift today, and the closest thing she had to a best friend. She hoped Cleo wouldn't look up from the TV when she slid into a seat at the table in the staff room.

"Finally, a minute alone." Cleo turned from the TV, giving Elysia an assessing glance. "Spill."

Assuming a cool expression, Elysia looked up from the newspaper spread across the table. "What?"

"Something's up with you. A man?"

"No."

Cleo laughed. "Yeah, sure. Only a man can make you as testy and disagreeable as you've been lately."

Frowning, Elysia met Cleo's eyes. "I don't know what you're talking about."

"I'm talking about that delicious firefighter you were banging for a short time. Suddenly, you no longer say a thing about him, and you're a regular grouch. Clearly, a lack of sex is to blame."

"Well, aren't you full of insights today?" Elysia glared at her.

Cleo nodded, asking matter-of-factly, "Did he dump you?"

Elysia inched up her chin. "No. As a matter of fact, he's madly in love with me." Why bother with the pretense? Cleo was the only person who had even an inkling of how her childhood had been, so she would be the only one who could understand why Elysia had rejected Nico.

Her green eyes sparkled with excitement. "That's fabulous. Are you keeping it hush-hush until you have a firm commitment?"

"No. I broke it off."

"What?" Cleo's outburst carried throughout the room, briefly rousing the interest of Rayanne, the doctor and owner of the women's clinic, before she returned to the latest medical journal she was reading intently. "Are you out of your mind? You finally find a man worth keeping, and you discard him?"

Elysia drew into herself, wrapping her hands around the coffee mug to draw some warmth from it, upon finding none from her so-called friend. "You know I don't want a man, not long-term anyway."

Cleo's voice lowered to a whisper when she leaned across the table, coming closer. "You aren't going to turn into your gold-digging mother or man-whore father by daring to have a relationship, Elysia. You don't really want to be alone for the rest of your life, do you? If so, it's a very bleak future you're contemplating."

She got to her feet, abandoning the coffee. "I'm happy as I am. I didn't ask for your opinion, and I'd appreciate you keeping it to yourself." Without allowing Cleo the opportunity to respond, Elysia swept from the staff room, refusing to look back or acknowledge the icy ball in her stomach that had formed at Cleo's words.

No, it wouldn't be bleak to be alone. It would be safe and predictable. No one could hurt her as long as she kept them all at arms' length. She regretted the friendship she had allowed to blossom with Cleo and vowed it would end right then.

IN KEEPING WITH HER decision, she met Cleo with a chill tone when the other woman stopped by the laboratory a little after four. "Yes?"

"I need to tell you something—"

"I accept your apology." She kept her attention focused on the microscope and her profile turned from Cleo.

"I'm not here to apologize."

Her distraught tone finally caught Elysia's attention, forcing her to look up. "What's wrong?"

"There's been a fire at the school...the roof collapsed." Cleo's eyes were wide with apprehension, and her hands trembled when she reached out to Elysia. "Two firefighters were killed, and three more have been taken to the hospital."

"Nico." Was he working a thirty-six-hour shift this week, or was it one of his three days off? She didn't know. Elysia didn't question her reaction as she dropped her briefcase and scooped up her purse, fishing for car keys as she ran to the door. Cleo shouted something behind her, but she didn't take time to figure out what it was as she ran through the building to the parking lot. She had to get to Nico. Please let him be alive.

THE HALLS AT SANDOVAL General were crowded with friends and family members of the firefighters, making it difficult for Elysia to push her way through the throng to the front desk. Three nurses engaged in various tasks ignored her for a long moment until she thumped her hand onto the counter to get their attention.

The oldest one looked up from her paperwork. "May I help you?"

"I'm here...is Nico..." She took a deep breath, struggling to compose herself so she could force out the question, almost afraid to hear the answer. "Is Nico Martin here?"

The nurse glanced at a clipboard before looking up. "He's in room one-eighteen."

Elysia turned from the desk, heading down the hallway.

"Miss, you can't go back there. Only family—"

She broke into a jog, hoping to outrun the nurse's admonishment and make it to the room before anyone stopped her. The woman's voice faded the farther away Elysia moved from the desk, and she dared to hope she would make it to the room.

She passed several rooms before seeing a man in a green security uniform moving toward her from the opposite end of the hall. Elysia increased her pace and pushed her way into one-fifteen as Security called to her.

Her breath caught in her throat when she saw the body lying in the bed, wrapped in bandages from almost head to foot. His leg was suspended in traction, and what visible skin there was around the bandages bore blisters. She walked forward, bracing herself. The person lying there was in bad shape.

"Nico." His name was a choked whisper, and she sagged forward, wanting to touch him but afraid of hurting him. "Oh, Nico, what have I done?"

"Elysia?"

She jerked with shock at his voice, spinning around to find Nico standing behind her. Her mouth dropped open, and she drank in the sight of him, noticing the bandages on his arm and across his forehead. She threw herself into his arms. "You're alive."

He held her close. "I wasn't inside when the roof collapsed. I got my injuries going in with the second squad to help get out my buddies."

Sobs shook her body, and she clutched his shirt. "I thought you were dying or dead. I was such an idiot." Elysia raised her head. "I could have lost you, and you never would have known—"

The door opened, admitting the guard. "You can't be in here."

Nico waved his hand. "We'll leave in just a second."

Elysia turned her head in time to see the guard's stern expression fade. "Never mind. I didn't realize she was with you, Nico." He turned to the door, leaving a heavy silence in his wake.

Finally, Nico cleared his voice. "You were saying?"

She hesitated, finding her courage had deserted her at the penultimate moment. During the frantic drive to the hospital, all she could think about was how could she go on without Nico, but now that he was safe, she found it impossible to remove the last fragment of the wall protecting her heart. Instead, she asked, "Who is the man in the bed?"

"My chief, Jim Carell. I'm waiting with him until his wife arrives. She works in San Diego."

"Will he make it?"

Nico sighed. "We don't know yet."

Still clutching his shirt, Elysia looked up at him. "What you do is dangerous."

He nodded. "Yes. I love it, but I'd give it up if you ask me to. I finally understand how my sister could walk away from her career for her wife."

Tears trickled from her eyes, and she buried her face against his chest. "I couldn't ask that of you."

He pushed up her chin, forcing her to meet his eyes. "Haven't you figured out by now I'll do anything for you? I love you, Elysia, more than I've ever loved being a firefighter. More than I've ever loved anything. I want to spend my life making you happy, if you'll let me."

The wall crumbled with what she swore was an audible crack. Elysia's muscles refused to support her, and she slumped against him, letting his T-shirt absorb her tears. "I love you, Nico." The words were strange on her tongue, but she meant them with every ounce of her being.

When she dared to look up, she found Nico's lips trembling and couldn't tell if his eyes were glazed with tears or if the mist was from hers. "I love you." This time, the words were easier to say. "I don't know how it happened or when, but I do love you. Can you forgive me for pushing you away?"

"It doesn't matter what happened in the past." His words carried significant meaning, not just for their history, but also for her own. "All that matters is the future."

She stretched on her tiptoes to kiss him, finding herself optimistic about the future for the first time ever. With the thawing of her heart, she was free to imagine a dizzying array of possibilities, and none were bleak. How could they be with Nico by her side?

About Mylia

IF YOU WOULD LIKE TO be the first to hear about new releases, please join my mailing list[1] and receive a free book. I love to hear from readers, so please feel free to email me at authormashton@yahoo.com.

---

1. https://subscribeto.eo.page/myliaashton

9 798223 506072